GIFFORD

First edition paperback
ISBN 978-1-915579-37-9

Gifford
Illustrations Copyright © David Hutchison. 2025

www.davidhutchison.info

Gifford

Prospectors Book 3

David Hutchison

Gert is cleaning the space spider's web off the Ariselle.

Esme and Flo watch from the roost station.

Gert: "Do you want any of this space spider web?"
Ahab: "No. Just bin it."

Gert dumps the web into the bin chute. He doesn't notice that a bit of web falls onto the floor.

Esme picks up the web.

Later, Esme wakes up in the middle of the night. She feels a bit funny and shaky.

Esme lays a huge egg which shakes and starts to hatch. Esme jumps off the nest. Flo wakes up.

A strange creature; a spider hen, hatches.

The spider hen looks up at Esme and squeaks: "Mama!"

Esme is scared and moves back.

The spider hen crawls out of the nest.
Esme flies off the shelf and out of the room.

The spider hen advances towards Flo. She flies off the shelf and follows Esme out of the room..

Flo and Esme rush down the corridor. They climb through a vent and hide in the air duct.

The spider hen scuttles past them.

The spider hen turns back and scuttles up to the vent.

The spider hen climbs through the vent and looks for the hens.

Round a corner the hens are hiding on a pipe above. The spider hen scuttles past then along the air duct.

The spider hen comes to the end of the air duct, smashes through the vent and climbs down into a storage cupboard.

Ahab finds the overturned nest and some scattered feathers.
Ahab: "Pip Pop, have you been chasing the hens again?"

The spider hen opens the lid of a tin and slurps tomato soup.

Tomato soup drips off the spider hen's mouth.
Ahab: "Oh no, that creature must have eaten Esme and Flo!"

A scared Pip Pop dashes off and clambers up into the bin chute.

Gert: "Pip Pop, you can't survive in space. Come back in!"

The spider hen rushes into the bin chute, and out into space.

The spider hen quickly spins a web and casts it to Pip Pop.
It hauls Pip Pop back to the Ariselle.

The spider hen helps Pip Pop through the air lock.
Pip Pop seems fine apart from her red eyes.

Ahab: "Oh thank you. You saved Pip Pop!"

Gert: "What is it?"

Ahab: "I think it's a cross between one of our hens and that space spider. I don't know how it happened, but let's call it Gifford."

Gert heals Pip Pop's red eyes with some eyedrops.

Ahab: "Aww. Gifford's made a hammock for Pip Pop."

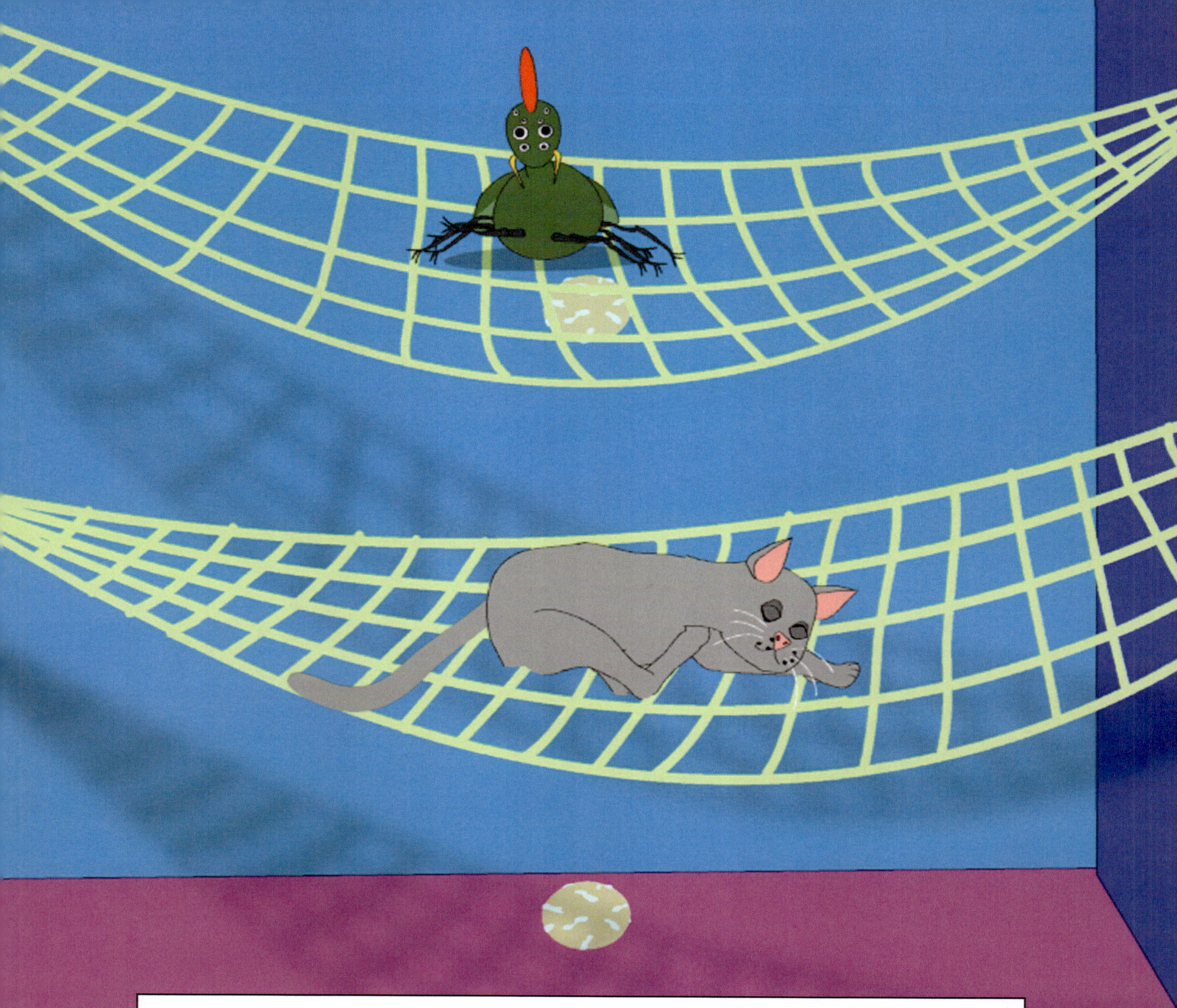

Later, in the middle of the night Gifford wakes up with a sore belly. Suddenly eggs start to pop out from her.

Pip Pop, Esme and Flo wake up. Gifford can't stop laying eggs.
Pip Pop dashes off to alert Ahab and Gert.

Ahab and Gert follow Pip Pop to the roost station.

Gifford has now laid a huge pile of eggs. Some of them start to hatch. The spider chicks squeak at Pip Pop.

Pip Pop rushes out of the room. The spider chicks follow her.

All the spider chicks follow Pip Pop to the storage cupboard.

Gert: "They're eating all our supplies!"

Ahab: "They eat metal too. We'll have to get them off the ship."
Gert: "I'll go and scan for a suitable asteroid."
Ahab: "Make sure that it's metallic, so that they have a food supply."

Gert: "I've found the perfect asteroid for them."
Ahab: "Great. How far away is it?"
Gert: "Just a few hours away."

They soon arrive at the asteroid, which is just as
well as the spider chicks are hungry for more metal.

Gert: "Hey you, stop eating the sliding door!"

Gifford says goodbye to her mum Esme.

Gifford says goodbye to Pip Pop.
Ahab: "I'm sorry Gifford but only you and your spider chicks can survive on this asteroid. We don't have time to build a station."

Ahab: "Good luck Gifford."
Gert: "Goodbye Gifford."

Gifford is sad as she and her spider chicks watch as the Ariselle blasts off.

Gert: "I'll miss Gifford but I've got a feeling that we'll meet her again someday."

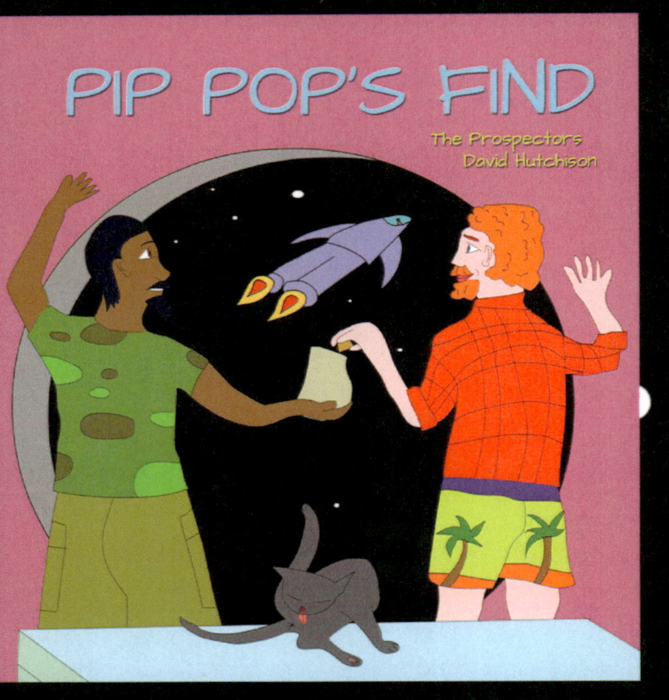

www.davidhutchison.info/theprospectors.html

9 781915 579379